This book belongs to

. . . .

D0309817

Copyright © 2022
make believe ideas ltd

The Wilderness, Berkhamsted, Hertfordshire, HP4 2AZ, UK.
6th Floor, South Bank House, Barrow Street, Dublin 4, D04 TR29, Ireland.

www.makebelieveideas.co.uk

Written by Rosie Greening.
Illustrated by Lara Ede.

The Wonky Gonks

Written by Rosie Greening • Illustrated by Lara Ede

Inspired by Andrea Bennet

make
believe
ideas

Here's a little secret
that grown-ups never tell:
we share this world we live in
with lots of GONKS as well!

Gonks are friendly, magic trolls
who use their gifts for good.
They help protect the planet,
just like everybody should.

The **Craggly Gonks**
love mountaintops;

the **Swirly Gonks** like seas.

But if you want the **Wonky Gonks** . . .

... you'll find them in the trees.

WONKY Wood

This **slopy, slanty, skew-whiff** crew all tilt off to one side.
They help take care of **Wonky Wood** and do that job with **pride**.

When a gonk is growing up,
they're always firmly told:
you'll get your **magic gem**
when you are 500 years old.

Giddy
age 400

age 300

age 200

Giddy age 100

The day had come for **Giddy**
and his friends to get a **gem**.

GONK GRADUATION DAY!

The eldest **Wonky Gonk** of all got up and said to them . . . .

"Use your gems **responsibly** to help **protect** the Wood.
If you **break** this **golden rule**, they **won't work** as they should . . ."

But Giddy barely listened to the **wise** things that were said.
He hid his gem beneath his hat and wandered off instead.

Through Fairy Glen,

Hi Giddy!

by Sparkle Glade

and past the **Blue Lagoon**,
Giddy waved to all his friends
and said, "I'll **see you soon!**

As his gem began to **glow**,
poor Giddy lost his head.
And in his great **excitement**,
he **forgot** what had been said.

"These trees will all
grow **chocolate drops**.

Perhaps I'll make it **snow** . . . .

These plants should all **blow bubbles**,

and this **grass** has got to go!"

But Giddy didn't notice how each wonky change he made caused the magic, glowing gem to . . .

slowly
dim
and fade.

Giddy **whirled** around the Wood to look at what he'd done.
And with a **gasp,** he realised the **cost** of all his fun.

The fairy trees were **ruined,**

the Lagoon was **frozen** stiff,

Giddy said, "I'll change it back –
your homes will all be fine."
But when he held his magic gem,
the jewel **refused** to shine.

Giddy ran by chocolate trees,
through bubbles, ice and snow.
He found the eldest Wonky Gonk

and cried,
"My gem
won't glow!"

The gonk said,

"You **forgot** the rule; the magic's **gone** for good.

You'll have to find **another** way to **clear up** Wonky Wood."

Giddy felt ashamed and said, "The Wood is ours to **share**.

I made it **worse** for everyone; from now, I'll take more **care**."

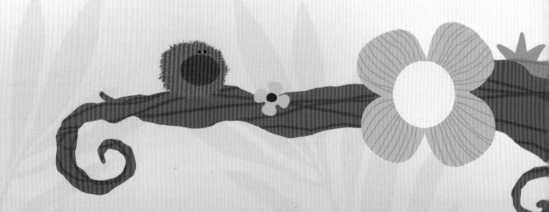

Giddy worked his socks off
from the morning 'til the night.

He **scrubbed**

and **sewed**

and **Popped** until he'd made the Wood look right.

From that day forward, Giddy was the **finest** gonk around.
He spread his wonky story, and he kept things **safe** and **sound**.

So Giddy learnt it's not just **gems** that help protect the Wood. Magic also comes from being **thoughtful**, **kind** and **good**.

This wonky world is **wonderful** and, though you may feel small, you have the **power** to keep it **safe** and **better** for us all.